bertha

and the Flying Bear

Story by **Eric Charles**
Pictures by **Steve Augarde**

from the original television designs by **Ivor Wood**

André Deutsch/Hippo Books

Published simultaneously in hardback by
André Deutsch Limited, 105-106 Great Russell
Street, London WC1B 3LJ and in paperback by
Hippo Books, Scholastic Publications Limited,
10 Earlham Street, London WC2H 9RX in 1987.

Text copyright© 1987 Eric Charles
Illustrations copyright © 1987 by
André Deutsch Limited and
Woodland Animations Limited.

All rights reserved
ISBN 0 233 97918 2   (hardback)
ISBN 0 590 70465 6   (paperback)

Phototypeset by Kalligraphics Limited,
Redhill, Surrey
Made and printed by Mateu Cromo,
Madrid, Spain

It was a sunny summer day. Inside the factory of Spottiswood and Company Bertha, the big machine, was hard at work making balloon bears.

As each one came down the conveyor belt, Roy checked it before TOM the robot took it to Nell who put it in a plastic bag and passed it to Flo to pack into a box.

Roy wiped his brow. "Phew!" he said, "It's hot in here."

"Boiling," agreed Nell, trying to push a bear into its bag. She pushed and pulled and then gave up. The bear was too big.

Flo was having trouble too. "This bear's too big for the box," she said.

"And this one won't fit into the bag," said Nell, "I think these bears are getting bigger."

Roy checked the next bear that Bertha made. It certainly looked bigger.
"Hey, Ted," he called, "The bears are getting bigger."

Ted stopped the machine and came to look. He picked up the bear and measured it. "You're right," he said, "I wonder what's making them grow?"

He went to the control panel and pushed the buttons, then pulled the lever and started Bertha again. "Let's see what happens with this one."

The next bear Bertha made was even bigger. Ted scratched his head.

"I don't know what's gone wrong," he said.

"The bear's very hot," said Roy. "Do you think that's got something to do with it?"

"Bertha's very hot too," said Ted.

"We're all too hot," said Nell. "The whole factory needs cooling down."

Ted pointed to the door to the factory yard. "TOM," he said, "open that door and let some air in, will you?"

The little robot scooted across to the big 'up and over' door. But couldn't find the handle to open it. "Peep – Peep," he cried.

"Roy, be a good chap and show him how the door works," said Ted.

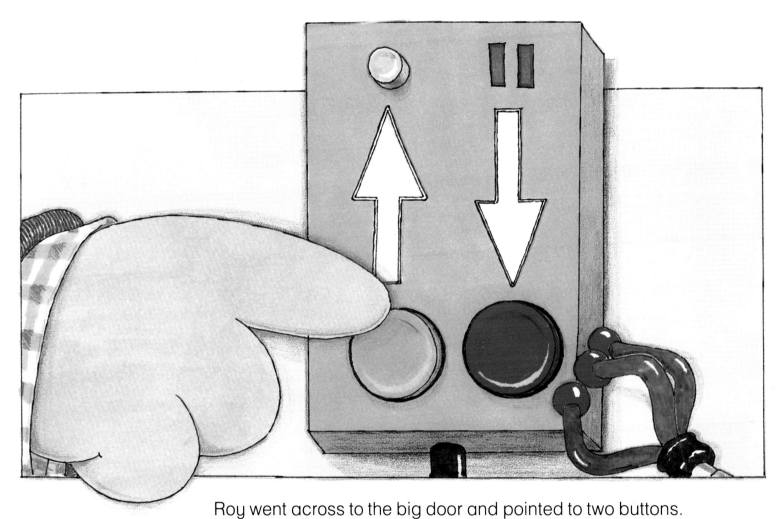

Roy went across to the big door and pointed to two buttons.
"You press this one to open and this one to close the door," he told TOM.
"Let me show you." OPEN – CLOSE. OPEN – CLOSE. The door swung up
and down as Roy pressed the buttons alternately.

TOM watched carefully, "Peep – Peep," he said, when he understood
and Roy let him press the buttons.

"That's a good idea," shouted Ted. "The door's acting as a fan."

"Making a nice breeze," said Nell.

TOM was delighted. The big door swung up and down as he pressed each button in turn. "Peep – Peeeep," he laughed.

"BEEEEEB!" Just as TOM pressed the close button – Panjid arrived in his fork-lift truck. There was a screech of brakes and a terrible BANG as the door slammed shut. TOM was so frightened that, without waiting to see what had happened, he scooted back to Bertha, leaving Roy to open the door.

An angry Panjid sat in the cab of his damaged truck. "Who's playing silly games with the door?" he asked.

Roy explained that it was an accident, and not really TOM's fault.

Panjid got down from the truck. "Goodness me!" he exclaimed, inspecting the buckled forks at the front. "That's some damage. I will have to fix it before I can move any more boxes." And he drove off to the workshop.

Roy left the door open and went back to Bertha. "It wasn't TOM's fault," he told Ted, "he didn't know Panjid was coming."

Mrs Tupp arrived with her tea-trolley. "Anyone for a nice cup of tea?" she asked.

"Too hot for tea," said Nell, fanning herself with her hand.

"I'd rather have something cold," said Flo.

"I'd rather have an ice cream," said Roy.

"That's a good idea, Roy," said Mrs Tupp, "I'll go and buy some."

The next bear Bertha made was huge. "Wow!" exclaimed Roy, when it came on to the conveyor belt. Ted came to look at it.

"It is far too big," he said. "Something's gone wrong. I'd better send for Mr Sprott."

When Mr Sprott, the designer arrived, he got out his measure and agreed that the bear was much too big for a balloon. "Let me see what I can do," he said, going over to Bertha's control panel and pressing the buttons. Bertha's lights flashed and her wheels turned. "That should do it," said Mr Sprott.

But he was wrong. The next bear was enormous. It was so big it flopped over the sides of the conveyor belt and stretched right down on to Nell's packing table. It was the biggest plastic bear anyone had ever seen.

"What *has* gone wrong, Mr Sprott," asked Ted.

Mr Sprott prodded the giant bear. "I think I know," he said. "This bear is

made of plastic . . . and when plastic gets hot it stretches. It seems to me that Bertha is so hot that the bears will go on getting bigger and bigger. You'll have to find a way to cool her down."

"BANG — CLANK!" agreed Bertha. Ted patted her.

"What shall we do with this giant bear?" said Roy, "We can't work with it lying there."

Mr Sprott studied the bear. "Well, if there are no holes in it, we could give it to a shopkeeper who's selling our bears to blow up and stand outside his shop as a sort of advertisement."

"Good idea," said Roy, "I'll just check it for holes." He fetched the air cylinders, fastened the line to the valve in the bear's foot and turned on the tap. As the bear slowly filled with air it took shape. It grew and grew, until it towered over everybody. Roy turned off the air and closed the valve. The bear began to rise.

"Don't let it float away," shouted Ted. Roy caught hold of its foot and held it down.

Mr Sprott gazed up at it. "My word!" he said, "That is the hugest bear I've ever seen."

At that moment Mrs Tupp arrived, her tea-trolley looking like an ice cream barrow. She had found a yellow parasol and set it at a jaunty angle. "Ices . . . Ices . . . Cornets . . . Choc Ices . . . Lollies!" she called.

"Oh, lovely," said Flo.

"Just what I need," said Nell, and went to find her purse.

"I'll have an ice lolly, Mrs Tupp," shouted Roy, and without thinking he let go of the bear and went across to the barrow.

"Watch out!" warned Ted as the bear began to float upwards.

Roy ran back but the bear was already out of reach. "Sorry," he said, "I forgot I was holding it."

The bear floated right up to the roof. Mrs Tupp looked up and saw it for the first time, "Goodness!" she exclaimed, "That's the biggest bear I've ever seen."

"It looks as if it's stuck on the ceiling," said Mr Sprott.

"We'll need a ladder to get it down," said Ted, "You'd better ask Panjid to bring the longest one he's got."

Roy sent TOM with a note for Panjid and everyone had an ice cream while they waited.

Presently, TOM and Panjid arrived carrying the ladder between them.

"That should do the job," said Ted. "Help me hold it steady, Panjid, so that Roy can climb up."

Ted and Panjid pulled the ladder into position and held it steady as Roy started to climb.

"Why are you climbing a ladder that leads nowhere?" asked Panjid.

Roy pointed to the roof. "To capture a flying bear," he said.

Panjid looked up and saw the giant bear stuck on the factory ceiling. "GOODNESS!" he gasped.

"That's the biggest bear I've ever seen."

When Roy reached the top of the ladder he stretched out, caught hold of the bear's foot and gave it a tug. The bear didn't move. "It won't come down," shouted Roy. "What shall I do, Ted?"

Ted thought for a moment. "Let the air out of it," he shouted back.

Roy reached up again and opened the valve in the bear's foot. There was a sudden hiss of escaping air and then a 'WHOOSH' as the bear shot away. Roy, caught in the blast of air, wobbled unsteadily on top of the ladder.

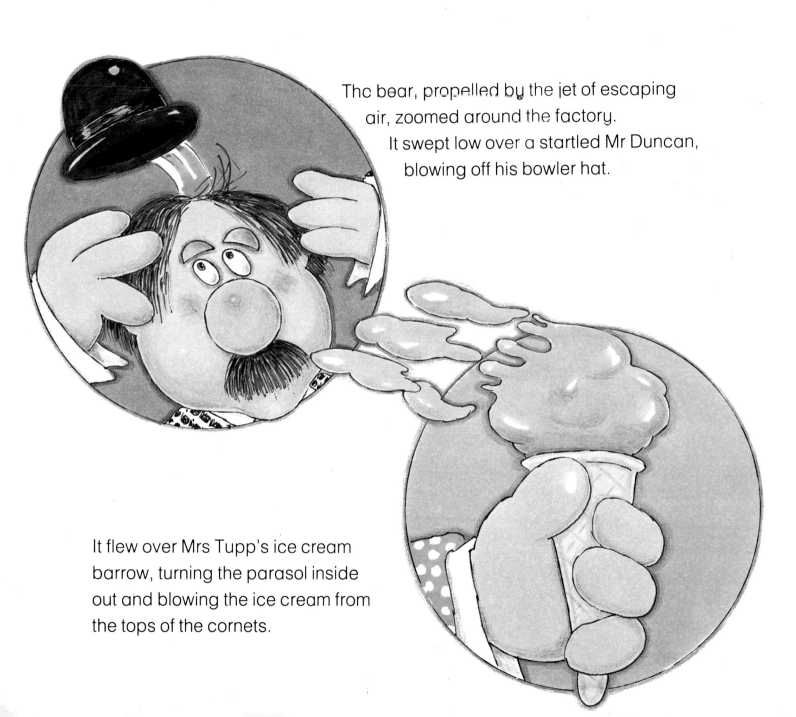

The bear, propelled by the jet of escaping air, zoomed around the factory.

It swept low over a startled Mr Duncan, blowing off his bowler hat.

It flew over Mrs Tupp's ice cream barrow, turning the parasol inside out and blowing the ice cream from the tops of the cornets.

It climbed high into the air again and zoomed towards the offices. Miss McClackerty was at her desk typing when the bear passed her window. She looked up, wondering why it had suddenly gone dark, and saw a huge bear.

"GOLLY!" she exclaimed and ran to the window.

Mr Willmake, the Manager, came hurrying out of his office. "What was that incredible thing that just went past my window?" he asked.

Miss McClackerty said, "It looked like a flying bear, sir."

"A FLYING BEAR!" cried Mr Willmake, excitedly, "What a wonderful invention. It's cooling down the whole factory." He ran out of the office, followed by Miss McClackerty. "Which way did it go?"

"That way, sir," said Miss McClackerty, pointing in the wrong direction.

The bear came around behind them and blew the Manager off his feet. "Wonderful! WONDERFUL!" he laughed. "So refreshing."

Roy was still clinging to the top of the wobbling ladder when the bear, suddenly appeared beside him. It hung there for a moment, grinning, and then, with a squirt and a faint 'whoosh', the last of the air escaped. The bear fell to the floor.

Everyone gathered round the crumpled heap. Mr Willmake shook Ted's hand. "A wonderful idea, Ted. The factory is much cooler now. How did you think of it?"

"I didn't, sir," explained Ted. "Bertha made it, Mr Sprott thought of blowing it up and Roy let the air out of it."

The Manager beamed with delight. "Well done, Roy," he said. "Well done, Mr Sprott, and WELL DONE BERTHA."